0.5

D1549084

MEET ALEX RODRIGUEZ

Baseball's Lightning Rod

John Smithwick

Published in 2007 by The Rosen Publishing Group, Inc.
29 East 21st Street, New York, NY 10010

First Edition

Editor: Jennifer Way
Book Design: Greg Tucker
Photo Researcher: Sam Cha

Photo Credits: Cover, pp. 1, 16, 14 © Ronald Martinez/Getty Images; pp. 4, 18, 29 © Jim McIsaac/Getty Images; pp. 6, 20, 30 © Al Bello/Getty Images; p. 9 © Otto Greule Jr./Getty Images; pp. 10, 13 © Tom Hauck/Allsport; p. 22 © Chris Trotman/Getty Images; p. 25 © Tasos Katopodis/Getty Images; p. 26 © Astrid Stawiarz/Getty Images for Gibson Guitars; p. 27 © Jed Jacobsohn/Getty Images.

Library of Congress Cataloging-in-Publication Data

Smithwick, John.
    Meet Alex Rodriguez : baseball's lightning rod / John Smithwick. — 1st ed.
        p. cm. — (All-star players)
    Includes index.
    ISBN-13: 978-1-4042-3636-3 (library binding)
    ISBN-10: 1-4042-3636-8 (library binding)
    1. Rodriguez, Alex, 1975– —Juvenile literature. 2. Baseball players—United States—Biography—Juvenile literature.   I. Title.
    GV865.R62S55 2007
    796.357092—dc22

                                                        2006019576

Manufactured in the United States of America

Contents

Alex Rodriguez is one of the Yankees' most popular players.

Meet Alex Rodriguez

You might know Alex Rodriguez better by his nickname, A-Rod. Rodriguez is the third baseman for the New York Yankees. He is a favorite among Yankee fans. He is also one of the most talented people ever to play baseball. Sports journalists describe the way that he swings and bats as perfect. A-Rod has the hits and the home runs to support this claim.

Rodriguez is just as good with his glove as he is with his bat. He has earned two Gold Gloves so far. The Gold Glove is an annual **award** given to the player who is the best at his position.

No baseball player has accomplished more than Rodriguez has in such a short time. He is already considered one of the best baseball players in the history of the game.

All-Star Stats

Rodriguez is one of the highest-paid players in baseball. He makes 87 cents every second. That's $3,132 every hour and $75,168 every day!

A-Rod has been playing baseball since he was a young kid.

Rodriguez's Childhood

Alex Rodriguez is Dominican American. He was born in the Washington Heights neighborhood of New York City on July 27, 1975. His parents, Victor and Lourdes, owned a shoe store. There were three children in the family, Alex, Joe, and Suzy. When Alex was four years old, the family returned to their native country, the Dominican Republic.

Victor used to be a catcher for a Dominican **minor-league** team. He taught Alex how to play baseball, and Alex fell in love with the sport.

In 1983, the Rodriguez family moved to Miami, Florida. Victor and Lourdes divorced, and Alex did not see his father for many years. Lourdes had to work two jobs to support her family.

Because his mother was often at work, Alex joined the Boys and Girls Club of Miami. The Boys and Girls Club is a national organization that provides guidance to children.

Alex continued to **excel** at baseball. He played for Westminster Christian High School, where he was also a star football player. In fact, the University of Miami offered him a **scholarship** to play both sports.

It turned out that Rodriguez would never play baseball or football at the college level. His skills had already drawn the attention of **professional** baseball teams. The Seattle Mariners **drafted** him after he finished high school in 1993.

A-Rod began playing professional baseball in 1994. Here he is signing a fan's baseball in 2005.

Rodriguez began playing with the Mariners in 1994. He posed for this picture in 1999.

The Seattle Mariners

By 1996, Rodriguez had become the Mariners' starting shortstop. This was a dream come true. When he was young, Rodriguez's baseball hero was Cal Ripken, the shortstop for the Baltimore Orioles. Now Rodriguez was a major-league shortstop himself.

The shortstop stands between second and third bases. The position requires a player with quick **reflexes** and a strong throwing arm. Most ground balls are hit in the shortstop's direction. The shortstop takes part in nearly every **double play**.

Rodriguez became a famous shortstop in his first starting season. His batting average of .358 was the best in the American League.

A batting average is the percent of hits a batter has per times at bat. If a player gets 10 chances to bat and gets 3 hits, his batting average is .300. A batting average is considered good if it is above

.280. A batting average higher than .330 is considered outstanding. By this measure Rodriguez's average of .358 was unbelievable.

In 1998, Rodriguez became only the third player in major-league history to join the 40/40 Club. A player wins this honor by hitting at least 40 home runs and stealing at least 40 bases in a single season. Rodriguez had 42 home runs and 46 stolen bases. His baseball career was only beginning, and he was already making history.

Rodriguez showed his skills for both fielding and batting while he played for the Mariners. Here he is during spring training in 2000.

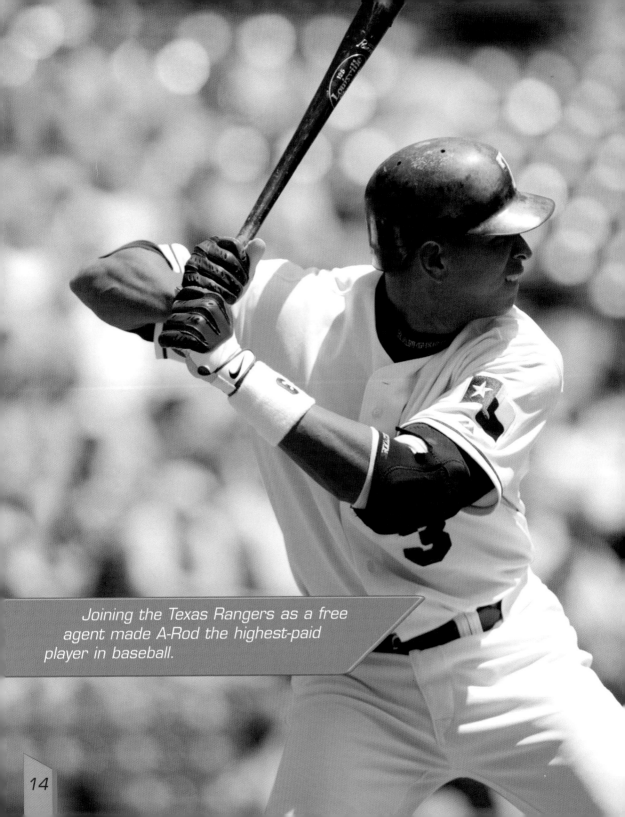

Joining the Texas Rangers as a free agent made A-Rod the highest-paid player in baseball.

The Texas Rangers

Rodriguez became a free agent after the 2000 season. A free agent can leave his current team and sign a contract with any team he wants to. This usually means a free agent will play for the team that will pay him the most.

The Texas Rangers finished the 2000 season in last place, but they had been an excellent team in earlier years. They wanted to improve, but they needed a star player. That star player turned out to be Rodriguez. The Rangers agreed to pay him $252 million over the next 10 years. This contract made Rodriguez the highest-paid **athlete** in America.

Rodriguez played even better in Texas than he did in Seattle. In 2002, he hit 57 home runs, the most home runs ever hit by a shortstop. While playing for the Rangers, Rodriguez won the Gold

Even though he had an excellent record with the Rangers, A-Rod's skills did not improve the team's standing. He moved to the Yankees in 2004.

Glove Award two years in a row. He was also the 2003 American League Most Valuable Player. This meant he was more valuable to his team than any other player in the league.

In spite of A-Rod's efforts, the Texas Rangers kept finishing in last place. The Rangers needed to fill their **roster** with other talented players. This meant they could no longer afford to pay Rodriguez. In 2004, they decided to trade him to another team.

The New York Yankees agreed to take Rodriguez. Since the Yankees already had a superstar shortstop named Derek Jeter, Rodriguez agreed to play third base.

When A-Rod moved to the Yankees, he had to change his uniform number. His power as an athlete did not change.

Before he played for the Yankees, Rodriguez wore the number three on his uniform. This was also the number worn by Yankee Babe Ruth, the most famous baseball player of all time. Out of respect for Ruth, the Yankees retired the number three many years ago. Rodriguez needed a new number. He chose unlucky number 13. It did not take him long to prove that old **superstition** wrong.

Many players struggle in their first season with the Yankees. No other team in baseball receives as much **media** attention and nationwide **scrutiny**. This can lead to a lot of **pressure**. Rodriguez dealt with the pressure. While his first season with the Yankees was not his best season, it was still very good. He batted .286 with 36 home runs. He also had 106 runs batted in. These are also known

All-Star Stats

Fellow Yankee Derek Jeter is one of Rodriguez's best friends.

Here is Rodriguez (left) with Derek Jeter (right), a Yankee teammate and one of A-Rod's closest friends.

as RBI. An RBI happens when a player on base scores as a result of the batter's hit. This was Rodriguez's seventh season in a row with at least 100 RBI.

In 2005, Rodriguez had one of his best seasons yet. He batted .321, hit 48 home runs, and collected 130 RBI. The highlight of his season came on April 26 in a game against the Los Angeles Angels. In just one game, he hit three home runs and contributed 10 RBI. Later that year he won his second Most Valuable Player award.

Rodriguez has become a valued member of the Yankees. Here he is helping his team beat the Mets, their hometown rival.

A-Rod off the Field

Alex Rodriguez is more than just a baseball player. He is also a family man. He married his wife, Cynthia, in 2002. Cynthia is a teacher. Their daughter, Natasha, was born in November 2004. Rodriguez says that he is prouder of his family than of any of his baseball accomplishments.

Rodriguez makes a lot of money, and he shares a lot of that money with charities. The Boys and Girls Club of America is one organization that benefits from Rodriguez. He remembers how the Boys and Girls Club of Miami helped him in his youth, and he is grateful. In addition to making large **donations**, Rodriguez hosts fundraisers to raise money for the club.

All-Star Stats

In April 2005, Rodriguez saved an eight-year-old boy in Boston from being run over by a truck.

Rodriguez has kept close ties with the University of Miami even though he did not go to college there. He gave the university $500,000 for the construction of the Alex Rodriguez Learning Center, a huge building that will be filled with computer labs, study rooms, and a large library. He created scholarships that allow students from the Boys and Girls Club to attend the University of Miami.

Rodriguez has also donated money to help out the Children's Aid Society, the New York City public school system, day-care centers in the Dominican Republic, and many other charities. Rodriguez is the richest athlete in America, and he is also one of the most generous.

Rodriguez enjoys helping the Boys and Girls Club. He is giving this Chicago Boys and Girls Club new computers.

This is Rodriguez and his wife, Cynthia, in 2005 at a party.

What's Next for A-Rod?

Even though he has been a successful player, there has been criticism, or bad talk, about Rodriguez's game. Some sports journalists say that Rodriguez is a poor clutch player. A clutch player is someone who performs very well under pressure, such as when his team is at risk of losing a game. While he has great averages, Rodriguez often plays best when his team is already winning and worse when his team is behind. This sometimes leads critics to wonder if Rodriguez is really worth his expensive contract.

In spite of these criticisms, Rodriguez is an accomplished baseball star. It did not take him very long to collect two Gold Gloves, two Most Valuable Player awards, 40/40 Club membership, the all-time home run record for shortstops, and more than 400 home runs. If his career continues to shine, the name Alex Rodriguez will be mentioned along with Babe Ruth and Ted Williams as one of the greatest

Here is A-Rod playing at Opening Day in 2006.

baseball players in major-league history.

Rodriguez began the 2006 season with a grand slam on opening day. A grand slam is a home run that is hit when the three bases are occupied, or loaded. This means that four runs are scored in a single play. That

Although he has many more years to play, Alex Rodriguez stands to go down in history as one of baseball's great players.

was a great way for Rodriguez to open the season, and it appears that his career will continue to shine for years to come.

Height: 6'3" (1.9 m)
Weight: 225 pounds (102 kg)
Team: New York Yankees
Uniform Number: 13
Date of Birth: July 27, 1975
Years in MLB: 12

2005-2006 Season Stats

Batting Average	Home Runs	RBI	Stolen Bases
.321	48	130	21

Glossary

athlete (ATH-leet) A person who takes part in sports.

award (uh-WORD) A special honor given to someone.

donations (doh-NAY-shunz) Gifts of money or help, contributions.

double play (DUH-bul PLAY) A play in baseball in which two players are tagged out.

drafted (DRAFT-ed) Selected someone for a special purpose.

excel (ik-SEL) To do something better than others.

media (MEE-dee-uh) Journalists and people who appear on TV and radio shows.

minor-league (MY-nur-leeg) Having to do with a group of teams on which players play before they are good enough for the next level.

pressure (PREH-shur) The weight of feeling worried about something.

professional (pruh-FESH-nul) Paid to do something.

reflexes (REE-fleks-iz) Actions that happen without thought.

roster (ROS-ter) A list of names, such as those on a sports team.

scholarship (SKAH-ler-ship) Money given to someone to pay for school.

scrutiny (SKROO-tuh-nee) Close observation, often to find mistakes.

superstition (soo-pur-STIH-shun) A belief that something is unlucky.

Index

Web Sites

Due to the changing nature of Internet links, PowerKids Press has developed an online list of Web sites related to the subject of this book. This site is updated regularly. Please use this link to access the list:
www.powerkidslinks.com/asp/alex/